'For Grace' – E.L.

'For my mum, Joan' – L.P.

OXFORD
UNIVERSITY PRESS

Great Clarendon Street, Oxford OX2 6DP

Oxford University Press is a department of the University of Oxford.
It furthers the University's objective of excellence in research, scholarship,
and education by publishing worldwide in

Oxford New York

Auckland Bangkok Buenos Aires Cape Town Chennai
Dar es Salaam Delhi Hong Kong Istanbul Karachi Kolkata
Kuala Lumpur Madrid Melbourne Mexico City Mumbai Nairobi
São Paulo Shanghai Taipei Tokyo Toronto

Oxford is a registered trade mark of Oxford University Press
in the UK and in certain other countries

First published in 2004

British Library Cataloguing in Publication Data available

ISBN: 978-0-19-272552-3

9 10 8

Printed in China
Colour Reproduction by Dot Gradations Ltd, UK

Paper used in the production of this book is a natural,
recyclable product made from wood grown in sustainable forests.
The manufacturing process conforms to the environmental
regulations of the country of origin.

Beautiful Bananas

Elizabeth Laird

Illustrated by Liz Pichon

OXFORD

UNIVERSITY PRESS

"Goodbye, Mama," says Beatrice. She's on her way to see her granddad. She's got a present for him. It's a beautiful bunch of bananas.

On the way, she meets a giraffe, who flicks his tufty tail. He whisks the bananas right off Beatrice's head and they land with a splash in the stream.

"Oh, I'm sorry," says the giraffe.
He picks some flowers, and
bends down low, and gives the
bunch to Beatrice. "My granddad
will like these," she says.

A swarm of bees settles on the flowers. "Hey!" Beatrice cries. She beats the bees off, but the flowers are crushed and spoiled.

"We're very sorry," say the bees. They wrap up some honeycomb, and give it to Beatrice instead. On she goes, down the path.

Some naughty monkeys see the honeycomb. "We like honey!" they cry. They snatch it away from Beatrice. All the honey drips on to the ground.

"Stop!" says Beatrice. "That honey was for my granddad." "Oh dear," say the monkeys. They run up into the trees and pick some mangoes for her instead.

Beatrice takes
the mangoes
and hurries on.

Suddenly, out jumps a lion! "Aaghh!" screams
Beatrice. She's very, very scared. She drops the
mangoes, and they all roll away.

"It's all right," says the lion. "I didn't mean to
frighten you." He pulls out one of his whiskers
and gives it to her. Beatrice runs on, holding the
whisker in her hand.

A parrot sees the whisker. He thinks it's a twig. He swoops down, and carries it off to build his nest. "Come back!" shouts Beatrice. "That whisker's for my granddad!"

"My mistake," squawks the parrot. He pulls a long feather out of his tail, and gives it to Beatrice. On she goes again.

But what's that long grey thing, dangling down beside the path? Beatrice doesn't see it. Accidentally, she brushes it with her feather.

"You're ti-ti-tickling me!" gasps the elephant.
"Atishoo!" His sneeze blows the feather away.

The elephant is sorry. He stretches out his
trunk, and picks a bunch of bananas. Beatrice
claps her hands. "Oh, thank you," she says.
"Bananas are best, after all."

Here at last is Granddad's house, and here at last is Granddad. "I've got something for you," says Beatrice, and she gives him the bananas.